Everyday
HEROES

For Ben Schoberle

LITTLE SIMON
An imprint of Simon & Schuster Children's Publishing Division
1230 Avenue of the Americas New York, New York 10020
Copyright © 2003 Mattel, Inc.
All rights reserved.
MATCHBOX™, MATCHBOX logo, and MATCHBOX HERO CITY™
and logo are trademarks owned by and used under license from Mattel, Inc.
All rights reserved.
READY-TO-READ, LITTLE SIMON, and colophon
are registered trademarks of Simon & Schuster. All rights reserved
including the right of reproduction in whole or in part in any form.
Manufactured in the United States of America
First Edition
2   4   6   8   10   9   7   5   3   1
The Library of Congress has cataloged the library edition as follows:
Library Edition ISBN 0-689-86147-8
Paperback ISBN 0-689-85899-X
Schoberle, Cecile.
Matchbox : everday heroes / by Cecile Schoberle ; illustrations by
Richard Courtney, Paul Lopez, and Joe Ewers.-- 1st ed.
p.cm. -- (Ready -to-read)
Summary: Brief rhyming verses describe a variety of trucks
in the community and the work that they do.
ISB 0-689-85899-X (pbk. : alk. paper) -- ISBN 0-689-86147-8 (Library Edition)
[1. Trucks--Fiction. 2. Stories in rhyme.] I. Courtney, Richard, 1955-ill.
II. Lopez, Paul, ill. III. Ewers, Joe, ill. IV. Title. V. Series. [E] --dc21

Everyday HEROES

By Cecile Schoberle
Illustrations by Joe Ewers & Paul Lopez

Ready-to-Read

Little Simon

New York London Toronto Sydney Singapore

Swish, swash!

Street sweepers wash.

Time to start
a brand-new day.

Honk, honk!

The tow truck comes.

It pulls the
car away.

Extra, extra!

The delivery truck stops.

It brings important news.

Ka-chink, ka-chunk!
Please move aside.

A garbage truck
is coming through.

Smish, smush.

Streets are full of slush.

The snowplow pushes snow.

The icebreaker scrapes.

What a team they make!

Now cars and boats can go.

Rumble, tumble.

Big dump trucks grumble.

They carry tons of dirt.

Churn, churn.

Cement mixers turn.

Be careful no one gets hurt.

Hurry, hurry!

No need to worry.

Big rigs can drive all day.

Tractor trailers carry cars.

Produce vans drive so far.

But the truckers
know the way.

Nighttime comes.

Power lines hum.

A bucket truck fixes a light.

Here comes a moving van.

It just rolled in.

There is a toy chest
and a bike.

Trucks help us every day.

They clean and carry.

They fix and load.

You can be glad
that everyday heroes
are on the road!